Shoebox Memories

Written by Helen Dineen

Illustrated by Marina Pérez Luque

Collins

1 A shoebox full of memories

Alex sat on his bed, unsure of what to do with himself. He glanced once more at the clock on his bedside table. The hands seemed to be moving much more slowly than usual.

He'd woken up extra early that morning, wolfed down his breakfast and dressed at the speed of light. But now he had nothing to do but wait.

His fingertips tapped on the bed, beating out
an impatient rhythm. One knee jiggled up and down,
unable to stay still. His breakfast sat uncomfortably
in his stomach and he wished he hadn't eaten quite
so fast.

The sky outside was brightening, but the world was
quiet and sleepy. From his window high above the city,
Alex saw a flock of birds take to the air over the tall
buildings on the other side of the street.

Alex rolled on to his stomach and reached under the bed, pulling out a battered shoebox. The lid slipped off as easily as usual and Alex carefully tipped the contents on to the bed.

There was quite a large pile. The familiar bright, shiny postcard, the encouraging letter, the email that he received just before his dance competition. Alex thumbed through the pages and smiled as he reread the silly jokes, which were still just as terrible. He stroked the ceramic seal, smooth and cool under his fingers.

As he read, the sky continued to brighten, and the roar of cars began to rise up to the apartment from the street below. Plates and glasses clinked in the kitchen as Mum and Sarah finished their breakfast and did the washing-up.

Sarah's voice floated through from the kitchen. "It's nearly time to go, Alex! You'd better hurry."

But Alex didn't hear his big sister. He was far away, lost in thought, reading and rereading all his shoebox memories.

Dear Dad:

FROM: Dad
To: Alex

5

2 Learning to dance

POSTCARD

15th January

Dear Alex,

Wish you were here! This is such a beautiful island, and the sea is really wild. Some of the waves are enormous. My cottage is very cosy, especially with the log fire, and the gloves you gave me are keeping me warm.
Write back soon,

Love Dad xx

1st February

Dear Dad,

Thanks for your postcard. Sarah stuck it up on the fridge with hers, so I can see it every day. Are there any interesting animals or birds on the island? I watched a documentary about seals at school today. Have you seen any of those? Do you feel cut off from the rest of the world? Do you even have a TV?

I hope the gloves are still helping. It's freezing here too – down below my window, people are scurrying like tiny little ants to get out of the cold. I hope it's going to snow!

Did Mum tell you I started tap dancing?
I've got special shoes with metal plates on
the bottom and on the heels, which make
a really loud noise as you dance. There are
names for all the steps – things like heel taps,
toe taps and shuffles. Next week, we're going
to start learning a dance routine. Do you
want me to show you sometime?

I'm going to use the shoebox that the shoes
came in to keep everything you send me.
I've found a spot under my bed to keep it safe.

Love Alex xx

From:	Dad
To:	Alex
Date:	12th February
Subject:	Back in the 21st century! 📎 seal.jpg

Hi Alex,

I've finally got the internet up and running, so I can email you now too! I don't feel quite so cut off from everything. I don't have a TV, although I can watch things online on my laptop now.

Brilliant to hear about your tap dancing. You must take after your mum because I have two left feet. I would love you to teach me, although I might look more like a penguin than a tap dancer!

Yes, we *do* have seals! Now I have email, I can send you photos. This seal dared to come up really close to me on the rocks this morning, when I was taking some samples of seaweed for my research. She has a large, dark grey blotch around her right eye, so I can tell her apart from the others. You can print this photo off and put it in your shoebox. What do you think I should call her?

Time for a quick joke before I go:

Why did the tap dancer have to give up? He kept falling into the sink!

Lots of love

Dad xx

From:	Alex
To:	Dad
Date:	20th February
Subject:	Re: Back in the 21st century! ✎cat.jpg

Hey Dad,

That's a terrible joke! But the picture of the seal is amazing. I think you should call her Fern. I can't believe you get to see seals in real life. There's nothing that interesting going on at home. Although Mrs Gumble from downstairs lost her cat yesterday and it turned up in our washing basket somehow! Sarah is annoying me as usual, but she says I'm just as annoying (SO not true).

I was at tap again today and we learnt to do a ball change. You have to step on the balls of your feet, first one then the other. We've been learning a dance for a few weeks now. There are loads of tricky steps to learn! I get frustrated sometimes. But then, when I get it right, it's the best feeling ever.

Well, I'd better go and help Mum set the table.
Macaroni cheese tonight – can't wait!

Love Alex xx

13

14

POSTCARD

10th March

Hi Alex,

Here's another postcard to add to the fridge. Try not to annoy your sister (I've told her the same!) and be good for your mum. Keep on tapping!

Love Dad xx

3 "Step in Time"

2nd April

Dear Dad,

It's been ages since I wrote you a proper letter. Everything's fine at school and Sarah and I are trying to get on better, I promise!

Actually, everything isn't fine at school at all. Can I tell you something? There are two girls in my class at school, Lily and Mina, who are also in my tap class. So, last week, we were talking about tap dancing at school and I was helping Lily with one of the steps in the playground.

Then some of the boys started being mean to me. Michael said dancing isn't for boys, and Lewis started twirling round like a ballerina. I wanted to go and hide in the toilets. I love doing tap but I'm not sure I want to do it anymore.

I do have some good news though – I'm going to be in the school football team! Mr Jones said my passing has improved loads this term.

Love Alex xx

From:	Dad
To:	Alex
Date:	9th April
Subject:	Chin up ☺ 📎 Bert.jpg 📎 skeleton.jpg

Hi Alex,

I got your letter this morning. I'm so sorry to hear you're getting teased about dancing. I wish I could give you a big hug. I had a look online last night and found some great videos of "Step in Time" from *Mary Poppins*. Have you seen it? Bert is a chimney sweep who tap dances across the rooftops of London with lots of other chimney sweeps. You'd be amazing as Bert. Boys definitely do tap dance – and do it brilliantly!

Congratulations on getting into the football team too – that's fantastic. I'm proud of you! Here's another Dad joke to cheer you up:

Why didn't the skeleton dance at the disco?
He had no body to dance with!

Was that as terrible as the last one?

Love Dad xx

From:	Alex
To:	Dad
Date:	12th April
Subject:	Dancing

Hey Dad,

Thanks for the email. Yes, your jokes are still bad! But they make me smile anyway. I was feeling really sad before I read your message, but I watched "Step in Time" online last night and loved it. One day, I want to dance on a big stage in a musical like that. Thanks. Got to go – Mum's getting cookies out of the oven and they smell amazing!

Love Alex xx

19th April

Dear Alex,

I can really see you on stage in a big theatre!
I'm glad you're feeling better about dancing.

Right now, I'm having a break with a lovely cup
of tea. It's very tempting to sit in this cosy,
warm kitchen for a while, but I'll have to get back
to work soon. The research is going well and I'm
getting some good results so far.

I can see a group of seals from the kitchen
window, lazing on the rocks. They look like they
are sunbathing, warming themselves after
a swim. Fern has claimed the biggest rock
for herself, of course!

Love from Dad xx

PS I thought you might like to see a map
of the island. It's a little bit like a fish,
don't you think?

North beach (perfect for seal spotting)

Harry the fisherman's cottage

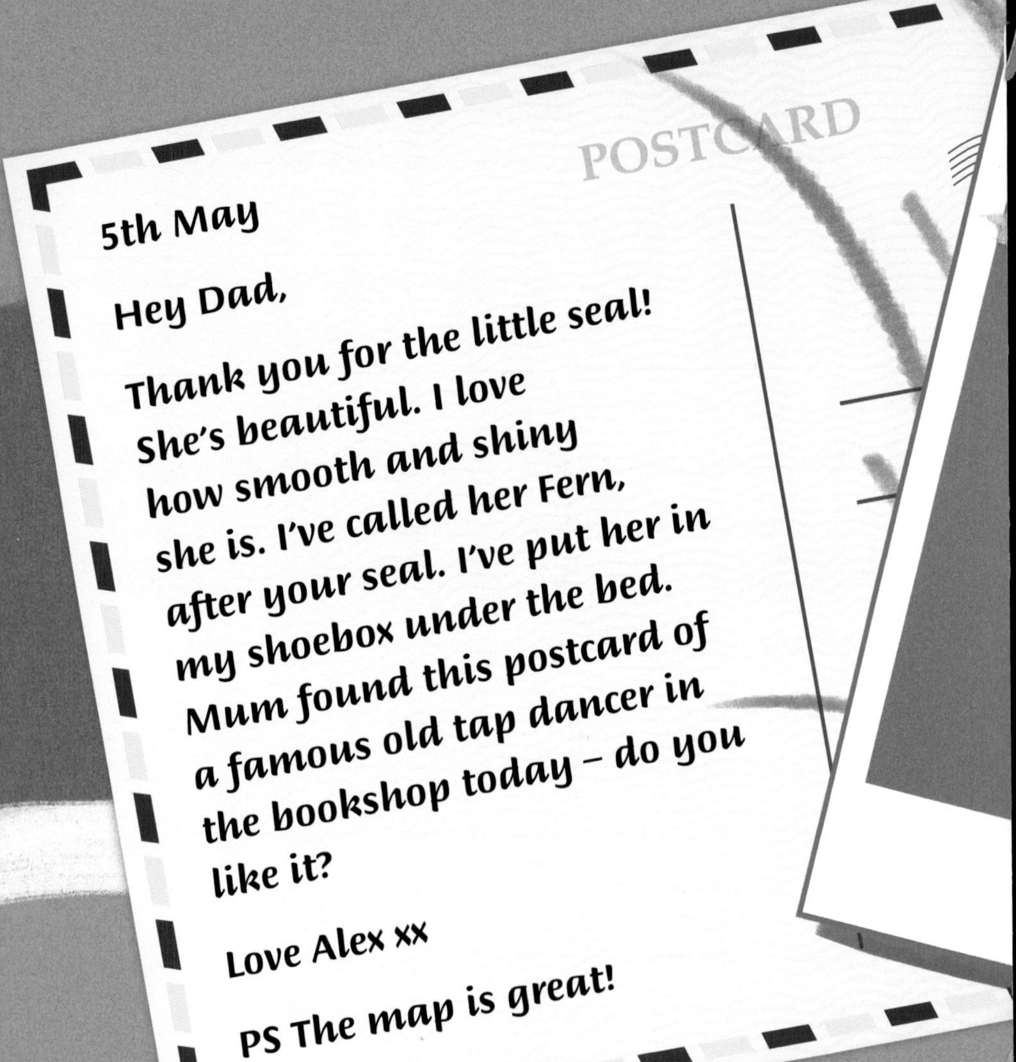

POSTCARD

5th May

Hey Dad,

Thank you for the little seal!
She's beautiful. I love
how smooth and shiny
she is. I've called her Fern,
after your seal. I've put her in
my shoebox under the bed.
Mum found this postcard of
a famous old tap dancer in
the bookshop today – do you
like it?

Love Alex xx

PS The map is great!

Fred Astaire

25th May

Dear Alex,

Thanks for the postcard. Fred was incredibly
talented and always looked the part too!
Do you ever get to wear such a cool costume
to dance in?

I've just come in from work and I've got sunburn
from being outside all day. I look as red as
a tomato.

It's been quite a day here. The pod of seals were
on the rocks sunning themselves this afternoon,
when I noticed Fern was off to one side,
looking uncomfortable. I crept closer and soon
realised she had some plastic twine around her.
The poor thing was cut around her neck where
the plastic was digging in.

I called over to Harry, who was fixing a fence
nearby, to see what we could do.

As we approached, the seals flopped back into the water, but Fern was caught by the twine on the rock and we were able to grab her.
She struggled to get away as she didn't know we were trying to help her. Luckily, Harry had some pliers with him, and he managed to cut the plastic away while I held Fern.

Fern was free! As soon as I let go, she slithered away into the ocean.

I hope she's all right – she gave us quite a scare. I'll be looking out for her. I've picked up so much rubbish that's been washed ashore and it's sad to think about the effect it has on wildlife. Maybe we can do something together to help.

Love from Dad xx

1st June

Dear Dad,

That's amazing! I'm so happy you rescued Fern. I can't believe you managed to cut the plastic and free her.

We've actually been learning at school about reducing plastic use and recycling as much as we can. My teacher Miss French set up a Green School Council and I've asked her if I can join. I'll tell everyone all about Fern so they can see why it's so important. I'll definitely take in that photo of her that you sent me.

Big news: I'm going to be doing a dance competition at the end of the month! I have to wear a bow tie, white shirt and a top hat, just like Fred Astaire. I've learnt so much more now – time steps, pick ups and cramp rolls.

I've been practising at home, but Mrs Gumble has been banging on the ceiling, so sometimes I go and practise in the school hall at breaktime. That's if Lewis and Michael aren't around.

29

Sometimes I think life would be easier if I didn't dance anymore. Even though I like both football and tap dancing, I don't like it when Lewis and Michael are mean to me at training. Maybe I should stick to football.

Love Alex xx

5 Time to shine

16th June

Dear Alex,

How is everything going? It was wonderful to speak to you on our video call yesterday, to see your smiling face and to show you and Sarah around the cottage.

I'm still trying to perfect the dance steps you showed me, but Harry falls about laughing every time I show him! I think you are definitely the best dancer in the family. All those rehearsals are really paying off.

Don't pay attention to what others think. Remember you have a talent that you love and make the most of it. Perhaps it's all new to Lewis and Michael and people can be unkind about things they don't understand. Once they know more about it, they are often kinder.

By the way, I found out something exciting this morning. Our friends the seals have had pups! They've been out on the rocks, sunning themselves again. And our old friend Fern was there too with her pup. Her neck is healing well after the scare we had with the plastic.

I'm so glad you're doing something at school about plastic pollution. People like you taking action will make such a difference to Fern and the rest of the marine life here. And hopefully, my research will help too!

Love from Dad xx

From:	Alex
To:	Dad
Date:	20th June
Subject:	School Talent Show

Hi Dad,

I had the best day at school today! It was the summer talent show and Miss French said I could do a tap dance in front of the class. My heart was beating really fast, but I thought about what you said about using my talents.

We moved all the desks to one side of the room so that there was enough space. It went really well, I remembered all my steps and at the end, I even got a round of applause!

Michael came up to me afterwards and asked me to show him how to do some of the steps.

"You make it look so easy," he told me, "but it's much harder than football!"

We had a football match after school and we lost 3-0, but I didn't mind too much because we played well as a team. Mr Jones thinks that next year, we'll have a real chance in the cup.

Now I need to focus on the dance competition – it's so close!

Love from Alex xx

From:	Dad
To:	Alex
Date:	22nd June
Subject:	Re: School Talent Show 📎 working.jpg

Hi Alex,

Well done for performing your routine at school! That's fantastic! Be proud of your achievements so far and keep working hard before the competition. I'm so proud that you didn't give up when you were being teased. Who knows, maybe next time Michael will be up there dancing with you.

Here's another dancing joke for you:

What do cars do at the disco? Brake dance!

Love Dad xx

PS My research project is almost finished. I can't wait to see you soon!

6 An exciting day

"Alex … ALEX!" Sarah's voice burst into Alex's room and his thoughts just before Sarah did. She was standing over him with her hands on her hips and an impatient expression on her face. But when she saw all the paper on his bed, her face softened.

"Come on, Alex, it's time to go. The taxi's here. We don't want to be late."

Alex rubbed his eyes as he came back to reality. He tucked all the letters, emails and postcards back into the shoebox, slid on the lid and placed it back in its special place under the bed. All his memories would be safe and sound. But he slipped the little ceramic seal into his pocket, the familiar smoothness soothing his nerves. Now he was ready to go.

"I can't believe it's finally time!" Sarah told Alex, eyes shining.

"I know – I can't wait," he replied. "I'm going to give him the biggest hug ever!"

For once, they both agreed on something.

Alex followed Sarah and Mum as the front door slammed shut behind them.

Then Alex burst back into the flat and ran to his bedroom.

"Just a second, I almost forgot it!" he yelled over his shoulder, before sprinting back out of the flat.

A few minutes later, the sound of a taxi engine roared into life below as it left the building, heading for the airport. Alex's room was quiet and tidy. Except for one short note which had fluttered down to the floor as he left.

Alex hopped from one foot to the other, scanning the stream of travellers coming through the double doors. Then ...

"*Alex! Sarah!*" Dad had spotted them, a huge smile spreading across his face.

"Dad!" Alex yelled.

As Dad dropped his rucksack to the floor, Alex sprinted towards him, arms open wide, clutching his dance trophy in one hand.

Dad was home and Alex couldn't wait to tell him every last detail. But for now, this hug was everything.

Alex's memories

Ideas for reading

Written by Christine Whitney
Primary Literacy Consultant

Reading objectives:
- discuss the sequence of events in books
- make inferences on the basis of what is being said and done
- predict what might happen on the basis of what has been read so far
- discuss and clarify the meanings of words, linking new meanings to known vocabulary

Spoken language objectives:
- ask relevant questions to extend understanding and knowledge

- use spoken language to develop understanding through speculating, hypothesising, imagining and exploring ideas
- participate in discussions

Curriculum links: Geography; Science – animals

Word count: 2893

Interest words: documentary, research, plastic twine, pollution

Resources: exercise book and pencils, ICT or non-fiction books for research about seals and pollution in the ocean

Build a context for reading

- Look closely at the front cover together. Ask children to discuss the illustration and comment on the two different settings. Why might two settings be shown?
- Read the blurb on the back cover. Ask children to predict what the challenges might be that Alex is facing at home.
- Challenge children to make connections between the contents of the shoebox, the title of the book and the *special person living far away* mentioned in the blurb.

Understand and apply reading strategies

- Read Chapter 1 together. Ask children to summarise what they think they know about Alex by page 5. Ask them to predict what Chapter 2 might be about.